The Things I **Love** About
Family

Trace Moroney

The Five Mile Press

I **love** my family,
and these are things
I love most . . .

my mother,

my father,

We do lots of things together and being with my family makes me feel safe and really, **really** loved.

They take care of me and understand my feelings.

Mum and Dad are good at helping me work out the right way to do things and how to make good choices. If I have a problem, I know they are always there to listen and help me.

Mum and Dad are also good at telling me when I do something wrong or naughty!

sorry

When I have been naughty I know that they still love me . . . but they just don't like my behaviour or what I did.

Mum and Dad help everyone in my family feel . . .

loved

accepted

a sense of belonging

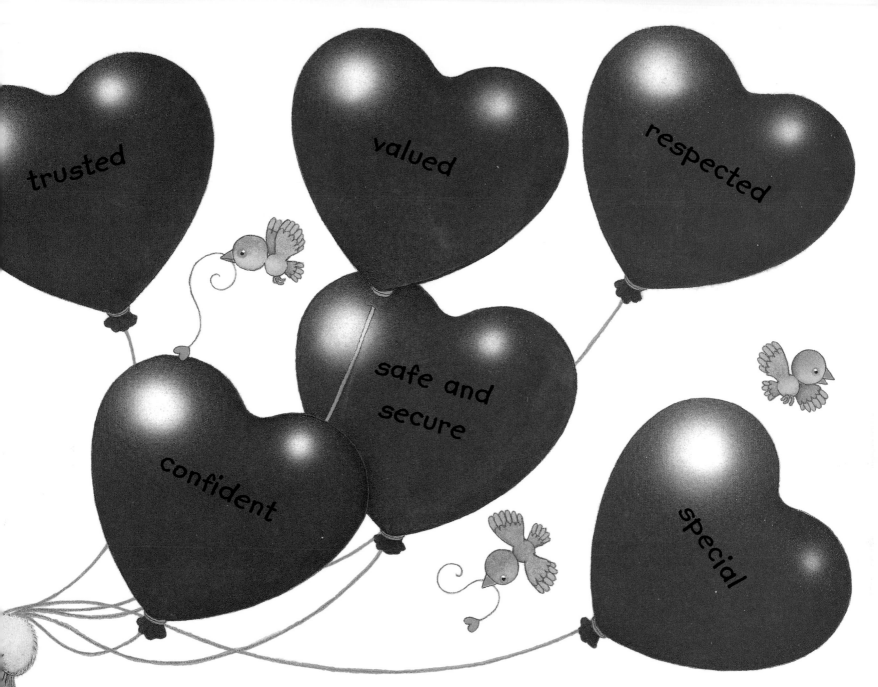

We talk about what these words and feelings mean, and different ways that we can **show** these feelings to each other.

Some families are really big . . .

some are middle-size . . .

and others are really small.

My family is part of a much larger family.
I have grandmothers and grandfathers,
aunties and uncles, and
lots and lots of cousins!

We often share special times together . . .
like Christmas dinner, picnics in the park,
and our famous family Easter-egg hunt!
I feel special being a part of my family.

Mum and Dad always tell me how much they love me and are proud of me . . . and give me lots of hugs! It makes me feel strong and more confident about **being me**.

I **love** my family.

In my family we always love and support
and care for each other – no matter what.
That's what makes us a family!

I **love** my family.

Notes for Parents and Caregivers

'The Things I Love' series shares simple examples of creating **positive thinking** about everyday situations our children experience.

A positive attitude is simply the inclination to generally be in an optimistic, hopeful state of mind. Thinking positively is not about being unrealistic. Positive thinkers recognise that bad things can happen to pessimists and optimists alike – however, it is the positive thinkers who *choose* to focus on the hope and opportunity available within every situation.

Researchers of positive psychology have found that people with positive attitudes are more creative, tolerant, generous, constructive, successful and open to new ideas and new experiences than those with a negative attitude. Positive thinkers are happier, healthier, live longer, experience more satisfying relationships, and have a greater capacity for love and joy.

I have used the word **love** numerous times throughout each book, as I think it best describes the *feeling* of living in an optimistic and hopeful state of mind, and it is a simple but powerful word that is used to emphasise our positive thoughts about people, things, situations and experiences.

Family

Family can mean different things to different people – but is most commonly defined as one of the following forms: two parents, one parent, blended, or extended. However, all families play a crucial role in helping a child feel a **sense of belonging** – primarily and most importantly within the family unit, but also in the world that surrounds them.

A happy, thriving family is a place where its members feel loved, valued, nurtured, heard and safe. It is also a place where one finds comfort, guidance, reassurance, encouragement and empathy. As parents (leaders of the family unit) we are responsible for imparting family values – and to do this effectively requires us to become an exemplary role model. In other words, we have to 'walk-the-talk'! The verbal and non-verbal messages children receive from us shapes the way they come to think about themselves – their self-worth.

Enjoyable family activities create opportunities for strengthening family bonds and relationships; affirming a sense of belonging; communication on a more playful and fun level; getting to know and understand each other (as family members grow and expand); and feeling more connected and 'plugged-in' to the family unit.

Make being a part of your family fun – be a parent your child will admire; earn your child's respect by being predictable in your own responses and behaviours; and spend time listening to your child's thoughts and feelings. You'll be amazed at what you learn about them . . . and yourself!

Trace Moroney

♥

In family life —
be completely present

Dare to Love

The Five Mile Press Pty Ltd
1 Centre Road, Scoresby
Victoria 3179 Australia
www.fivemile.com.au
Part of the BonnierPublishing Group
www.bonnierpublishing.com
Illustrations and text copyright © Trace Moroney, 2010
All rights reserved
www.tracemoroney.com
First published 2011
This edition 2013
Printed in China 5 4 3 2 1
National Library of Australia Cataloguing-in-Publication entry
Moroney, Trace
The things I love about family / Trace Moroney.
9781742480572 (hbk.)
9781742484815 (pbk.)
For pre school age.
Families--Juvenile literature.
A823.3